UNLIKELY WITNESS

AMISH MYSTERY ROMANCE

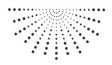

GRACE GIVEN
PURE READ

D1315518

A PERSONAL WORD FROM GRACE

66 Thank you, dear reader, for choosing to pick up one of my stories. I love to write and bring characters and sweet stories to life, and I am truly humbled that you are sharing the journey with me.

God bless you as you read.

With much love,"

Grace Given

Grace Given (Author)

THANK YOU FOR CHOOSING A PUREREAD ROMANCE.
AS A WAY TO THANK YOU WE WOULD ALSO LIKE TO
GIVE YOU A BEAUTIFUL EXCLUSIVE STORY BY GRACE
GIVEN, PLUS SOME OTHER GOODIES.

Click Here To Download Your Copy of Grace Abounding

2

CITY EXPERIENCES

Abigail bent to scoop the dust into the dustpan and then emptied it onto the hard ground near the woodshed. She looked at the azure sky and praised God for the works of nature that surrounded her. The Amish woman asked God to give her mother a pain-free day. Miriam Bontrager suffered from Multiple Sclerosis and could no longer carry out the duties of an Amish wife and mother.

"Abigail, I want to wash Maem's face. Is that all right with you?" Ten year old Mary waited for her sister's answer. Abigail smiled at her.

"You may do that today. Don't get the water too hot on the cloth."

At age 18, Abigail slowly began to feel as if she was the mother to Mary and the other children. Her twelve year old sister Ruth helped with many of the chores but soon both girls would return to school for fall classes. Her brothers Aaron, age 16 and Zeke, age 19 were kept busy helping her father with necessary chores on the large farm. Zeke was engaged to be married in a few months. Abigail often thought of Seth Weaver and didn't miss his glances that came her way when in social gatherings and even during church services. She wished she could return his attentions but her mother's care came first.

Dust billowed from beneath a horse's hooves and Abigail smiled when she saw her best friend ride up. Rebekah Zook quickly got off her horse and walked toward Abigail.

"Mr. Johnson has sent word the General Store is ready for our quilts. Maem just finished the last stitch in the Log Cabin one. Do you want to go into Valley Falls with me?"

The two women came through the kitchen doorway and Miriam heard Rebekah's question.

"You should go with her, Abigail. It will be a gut break for you. Ruth and Mary will take care of me." Miriam gestured toward her two youngest daughters. Both stepped forward, eager to help care for their mother.

The last thing Abigail wished to do was to go into the town filled with strange sounds and noisy Englischers. She preferred to take her rare breaks walking around her father's farm. She liked to study nature as it rotated thru the seasons. It was the perfect time and place to connect closely with God.

Rebekah grabbed her friend's hand. "Go get ready, Abigail. I'll ride back home and get the quilts and the buggy."

When her friend left, Abigail sent pleading looks toward her mother.

"I know how you feel about going into town, Abigail. But

when you have your own home you will have to do that to purchase things you won't make or grow."

Miriam's eyes swayed Abigail. Miriam was aware that her eldest daughter should be enjoying a serious courtship by now. Seth Weaver was an upright Amish man. He had an even temper and good humor. Miriam knew that if she didn't have to depend on Abigail for her care that Abigail would be anticipating her wedding day. Abigail wanted to please her mother. She verbally agreed it may be good practice for her to go along with Rebekah.

On the way into town, Rebekah spoke of her courtship with Gideon Hanson. They, along with Abigail and Seth had been baptized several months previous. Rebekah hoped Seth would get the courage to ask Reuben Bontrager for permission to court his daughter. Abigail needed normalcy in her life, thought Rebekah.

"Gideon has enlisted several members of the community to build our house. His Daed has given him twenty acres for us to begin our life on."

"That's wonderful, Rebekah. Gideon is a fine man and I know you will be happy."

"It's about time Seth asked to court you, Abigail. I don't know what he's waiting for."

A faint tint of pink covered Abigail's face. "I don't have time to be courted by anyone, Rebekah. Every day I see my Maem fail more. She keeps a cheerful attitude but I know she suffers greatly." She paused and watched the sheep grazing beyond the fence. "I do like Seth but he hasn't approached my father. He may be interested in someone else. I doubt he wants to wait for me."

Rebekah shook her head vehemently. "He loves only you, Abigail. Everyone can see that in his eyes. He's just too weak to step forward. I think I'll ask Gideon to prod him along for you."

"Oh, no, Rebekah," Abigail said, "that is too forward. If he wants to take me for buggy rides he will do it in his own time."

Abigail had mixed feelings when she saw the edge of Valley Falls. She wasn't sure if she was dismayed the subject of Seth was interrupted, or dreaded going into the crowds of the bustling town. The latter would probably prove to be the worse option for her.

"I want to visit the shops once I sell the quilts to Mr. Johnson. His wife Lisa is so nice and always tells me that she is sure every quilt will sell."

Randall Johnson smiled when he saw Rebekah Zook walk in with Abigail. He told one of his stock boys to go out and bring the large bundle of wrapped quilts inside. The Englischer greeted the women and Lisa offered them a hot cup of coffee. Both thanked her but declined.

While Rebekah dealt with prices and the quality of the quilts, Abigail allowed her eyes to move around the store. The shelves filled with every possible food brand. She wondered why the Englisch didn't have gardens and can their own vegetables and fruits. Her eyes landed on the back corner of the store where bolts of material lined three short aisles. Abigail took a step forward and looked in wonder at the varied colors and designs. Caught up in her reverie, she was jolted back to her surroundings when a rough shoulder rammed hers.

"Get out of the middle of the aisle," a surly voice commanded.

"I'm sorry." Abigail stepped closer to the counter where Rebekah negotiated.

Randall Johnson stopped what he was doing and glared at his son Tyler. He had been taught the same good manners as his two sisters and younger brother, and yet Tyler at age 26 still did nothing but cause chaos and trouble toward everyone he came in contact with. The quiet Amish woman was no exception.

"I apologize for my son's behavior," Lisa told Abigail. Tyler lived independently and moved from one job to the next. His companions consisted of several around his age who often, along with Tyler, faced the Law for petty crimes committed. "Are you all right?" Abigail appeared shaken.

"I am fine," she said. "I was standing too far into the aisle and there was little room for anyone to pass by."

Lisa and Randall exchanged frustrated glances and then returned to the business at hand. Abigail hoped the transactions would be completed soon. The atmosphere in the store suffocated her. At last, Rebekah turned to her with sparkles in her eyes.

"I have a short list of things needed at home."

Abigail followed her to the back of the store while Rebekah pointed out a sack of flour and one of rice to the clerk in that department. Abigail recalled their sugar bin was almost empty and she bought a large bag of it. The man took the items to the buggy. Rebekah covered the items with the woolen blanket and then turned to Abigail.

"I want to show you some pretty things in a window a few

stores down." They stopped in front of a jewelry store. "Just look at the gems." Rebekah then suggested they go inside and see what else was in the store.

"We can't buy trinkets like that. Besides, why are we even looking at such things?"

Rebekah laughed at Abigail. "It won't hurt us to take a look. I can't imagine wearing something like that around my neck or wrist but you have to admit they are beautiful."

The woman behind the counter came forward. She explained most of the jewelry was handcrafted. Abigail's interest was piqued when she mentioned stones found in nearby creek beds.

"Of course, those aren't high dollar," the clerk said, "but there are a few artists around town that like to create using materials from nature. The other pieces are real gems."

The Amish women admired the workmanship. Abigail was anxious to leave the store. If an Amish person saw them coming out, they would be reported to the Bishop. Abigail tugged gently on Rebekah's arm.

Once outside, she drew a deep breath. "I hope none of our neighbors are in town to see us," Abigail said.

"We didn't buy anything in there. I don't believe there's any shame to just look." Rebekah pointed out the Ice Cream Shop. "Let's get some ice cream."

"That sounds like a gut idea," Abigail said. "Then I should get back home. I don't fully trust Mary and Ruth to care for Maem's needs."

Rebekah agreed the Ice Cream Shop would be their last stop. She gave up trying to relax her good friend and accepted

Abigail's nervous nature. They ordered cones. Rebekah opted for chocolate and Abigail chose strawberry. They sat at a small table near the window and each enjoyed her treat.

Suddenly boisterous voices filled the small space. Tyler Johnson burst in with his best friend Matt Kilgore. They repeated a crude joke and laughed loudly. A young boy approximately eleven or twelve years old tagged along behind them.

"Go back to the store, Tim. How many times have I told you not to follow me every time you see me on the street?" Tyler's voice held contempt.

"I'm not following you. I just want some ice cream. Will you buy me some, Tyler?"

Tyler looked down on the boy. "Why would I do that? Just get out of here. I don't need a kid brother following me all over town." His words were followed by choice curse words.

Tim didn't appear fazed by his older brother's actions. He stood where he was as if he expected Tyler to buy the treat for him.

"I guess the only way to get rid of you is to kill you, Tim. How's that sound to you?"

Tim shrugged and finally gave up. He turned and left the Ice Cream Shop. Abigail saw him almost skipping down the street and had to admire his courage against his older brother.

The clerk took the young men's orders. Tyler leaned on the counter and leered at the young girl making his milkshake. The words he used caused Rebekah and Abigail to cringe. Matt's low laughter emphasized the meaning. Rebekah tried a conversation for distraction but the words spilling from the men's mouths weren't overridden easily. To the relief of everyone in the shop the two left just as unruly as they had entered. The Amish women waited until they disappeared down the street.

"Even I'm ready to get home again to peace and quiet," Rebekah said. Abigail agreed without reservation.

With each of the three miles becoming a distant memory behind them, Abigail visibly relaxed. Her eyes lit up when Rebekah turned the buggy into the Bontrager lane. She slowed the buggy when she saw a familiar horse with its reins looped over the hitching post.

"That looks like Seth's horse," Rebekah said. She grinned. "Maybe he's finally got the courage to speak with your father."

Abigail's heart flip-flopped. The tall muscular man stood talking with her brother Zeke. Seth's light brown hair was shining in the mid-afternoon sunlight. The conversation appeared a serious one. When Abigail got down from the buggy she started to unload her bag of sugar.

"Don't do that, Abigail. Wait for Seth and give him the opportunity." Rebekah smiled. She schemed to get the two into a conversation together.

They walked toward the house.

"I'll join the others to build the Hanson house," Zeke was saying. He noticed Rebekah. "We were just talking about you. Seth is asking for more help to build the house for you and Gideon. I'll help and I'm sure Aaron will, too."

"Thank you. It should go fast now that workers are lined up."

Seth looked at Abigail and finally found words to greet her.

"Zeke told me you had gone to town with Rebekah. I hope you had a gut time."

"I didn't, but it's because Valley Falls isn't my favorite place to go. Maem and Rebekah thought it would be gut for me to get away for a while."

Everyone in the group knew how attached Abigail was to her home. Even if Miriam didn't need the care, Abigail would rarely leave her Amish surroundings for town. Seth smiled at her.

"At least you are honest about it," he said.

Aaron and Reuben walked into the yard and joined the group. "Do you need help unloading anything?" her father asked. The young men jumped to the rescue and voiced their offers.

"I just have a bag of sugar. I noticed this morning that our bin was just about empty."

"Seth will get it for you." Rebekah decided before anyone had the chance. Seth quickly obliged.

Zeke looked at his father. In a low voice, he asked, "I wonder how long it will take Seth to ask to court my sister."

Reuben shook his head and smiled. "I keep thinking he'll get his courage up at any time but so far it seems he just can't muster it. I'm surprised at that since he is a take-charge young man."

"He needs someone to give him a jab in the right direction," Aaron said. He watched Seth glance at their sister more than once as he carried the sack of sugar to the back porch.

Miriam called to Seth. She sat in her wheelchair in the kitchen and wondered what the men had been talking about.

Ruth poured hot tea into her cup. By getting Seth's attention, Miriam knew Abigail would follow him in to check on her. Abigail thanked Rebekah for the outing and went inside.

Seth removed his straw hat and greeted Miriam. She invited him and Abigail to sit for some tea. Ruth sliced banana bread and put the plate on the table. Aaron, Zeke and their father came inside.

"That banana bread smells gut," Zeke said. "We're ready for a bite of it."

The family talked about the chores completed and the ones yet to do before nightfall. Abigail asked how things had gone at home while she was in Valley Falls.

"I had very gut care. My two girls spoiled me," Miriam said.

Ten minutes passed before Seth spoke directly to Abigail. "Did you have time to get a treat at the Ice Cream Shop, Abigail?"

A dark cloud fluttered across her face before it disappeared and her cheerful countenance reappeared. "We each had an ice cream cone. It was delicious."

"That was one gut thing about town then," Seth said. His eyes twinkled in a teasing manner.

"It was gut and we were ready for it. Rebekah did very well with the quilts at the General Store. The Johnsons made room for them before we left."

"Rebekah and Anna sew beautifully. I've never seen a stitch out of place by either of them," Miriam said.

Seth shifted and opened his mouth to speak and then decided against it. Then he stood up and tried again. He took a deep breath.

"I must be leaving now," he said. He thanked Ruth for the bread and then spoke to Abigail. "Would you mind walking out with me, Abigail?"

She steadied her cup before it toppled and followed him.

The family members nodded at one another after they went outside.

"Is Seth going to marry Abby?" Mary asked.

"That is very possible, but not today," Miriam told her.

3
CHANGES

Reuben Bontrager noticed his eldest daughter's fatigue. Since the day Seth Weaver invited her to walk outside with him, Abigail seemed dejected. She clipped the last clothespin onto the towel and snapped it onto the clothesline.

"Abigail, I feel your duties are too much for you. Perhaps we should find a way to give you more help with your Maem. Ruth and Mary will begin school again in a week and then everything will fall on you."

Before Abigail could answer, a buggy arrived. Their farm neighbor to the south got down from the seat. Reuben and Abigail greeted Amos Graber. He responded and then Amos spoke to Abigail.

"I know you have plenty of work to do right here, Abigail, but my wife Sarah has broken her wrist and asked if you might help cook our noontime dinner. It will only be for a week or two at most. She is anxious to do her own work again. Lissa works for several hours in the middle of the day assisting her grandmother or she would do it."

Reuben knew his daughter would do anything for anyone in need and this was no exception.

"I suppose I could come over once I have our dinner on the stove. Ruth is old enough to watch it and serve it. She and Mary will soon be in school and then I'm not sure how much I can help. My Maem will need me full-time without the girls around."

"Thank you, Abigail. Even extra help for one week will be gut."

When Amos left, Reuben looked at his daughter. "Perhaps you can ask Rebekah to help one week. She may be free to come here or take over tasks Sarah Graber can't do right now."

Abigail nodded. She felt sure Rebekah would help.

"Dr. Andrews in Valley Falls will be seeing your Maem again," Reuben said. "I will take her in. I hope he will be able to relieve her discomfort some."

"I do, too, Daed. Don't worry. We will get along fine even if things get busier."

When Reuben went into the house, Abigail's thoughts went back to the day Seth asked her to walk with him to his horse. She fully expected him to ask to court her. Instead, he talked of incidental things that made no sense to Abigail. His mannerisms told her he had no plans to wait for her. Even Abigail doubted she would ever be free to allow courtship by Seth or anyone else for that matter. He didn't have to speak words of rejection since he failed to even touch on the subject.

At dinnertime Reuben announced the change in routine. He explained Sarah's accident. Miriam frowned. "I'm sure there are plenty of our friends who will take turns with her duties until her wrist heals. Why didn't Amos send word around?"

"I believe it is because he knows our daughter never says no to anyone in need."

"I will rely on Ruth and Mary for a couple of hours," Abigail said. "It will only be for one week. I believe that everything can be managed." Her younger sisters eagerly agreed.

"Don't forget there is the church picnic coming up at the end of the week," Miriam said. "That means more cooking right here to get dishes ready to take along."

Abigail had forgotten the upcoming end-of-summer picnic. "We will make potato salad and slaw. Ruth, you will slice the potatoes and place them in cold water two days before the Saturday picnic. Then Maem will tell you the other ingredients and how to mix it into a salad."

"What do you want me to do, Abby?" Mary waited.

"You will shred cabbage for the slaw."

Miriam realized how much Abigail took control of things she should be doing. Abigail noticed her mother wasn't smiling.

"I mean those are your jobs if Maem approves. She may have other ideas for you two."

Miriam smiled. "I think those jobs are perfect for Ruth and Mary. I will help by teaching them how to put it all together."

The rest of the day was filled with needed chores. Miriam rested in bed most of the afternoon. That evening when prayers ended, Reuben told Miriam and Abigail he wanted to speak in private with them. The others headed for bed and Abigail and her parents sat back down.

"I believe when you see the doctor tomorrow, Miriam, that we should ask him if he knows of a nurse to come in and assist you. I feel Abigail needs help." He held up his hand when his daughter started to protest. "I know of other Amish families who over the years have accepted services from Englisch nurses. I will get the approval of Bishop Wirth and go from there."

Early the next morning, Reuben left to visit the Bishop who gave his approval. He returned home and made his wife comfortable in the buggy before starting for town. Abigail had mixed feelings that her load may be lightened and wondered what it would be like to have an Englisch nurse in their Amish home daily.

When her parents returned from Dr. Andrews' office, Reuben told Abigail it was settled that a nurse would arrive the next day. "Her name is Nancy Sinclair. She is twenty-four and is married. She has cared for Amish patients in the past and comes highly recommended. Abigail, you show her the daily routine and allow her to perform her duties in caring of your Maem."

"I am happy for the extra help for you, Abigail," Miriam said. "Once she knows the routine you have set in place, you will not be so overworked."

Abigail's nerves were on edge the day Nancy Sinclair was to arrive. She continually looked out the window until she saw a tan car stop at their house. A slender woman with dark hair carried a bag with her and approached the front door. Abigail welcomed her in. She then introduced her to her mother. Ruth and Mary stood in the kitchen doorway and watched.

"These are my youngest daughters," Miriam said. "This is Ruth and the younger one is Mary. They have been gut helpers but will soon be returning to school."

Nancy smiled and praised the girls for helping their mother. Abigail and Miriam invited Nancy to sit down and they discussed the routines they had been following. The nurse told them they had it worked out well. She glanced at the clock and according to Abigail's schedule it was time for Miriam to rest in bed. She assisted her into bed and asked if she needed anything else. Miriam's eyes fluttered and she shook her head no.

When Abigail joined Nancy in the sitting room, Nancy explained the medicines her mother was taking. For the first time, Abigail understood the reasons for each of them.

"If you have other duties, I can either help you or study your mother's medical history."

"I will do my work while you learn about my Maem's condition," Abigail said. "She usually rests for an hour or sometimes forty-five minutes and then likes to join the family. When she gets up she is given two of these pills." Abigail pointed to the prescription bottle. Nancy assured her that once Miriam was up again, they would work together until Nancy knew the routine.

In two days, the church picnic would occur. Abigail helped Ruth and Mary prepare food while Nancy fell into the customary care of her mother. Abigail always looked forward to celebrations in her Amish community. This time she was apprehensive how Seth would interact with her. She prayed he didn't show interest in another Amish girl. Several young women hoped he would notice them.

Abigail finished at Sarah Graber's house and hurried home. She knew she should check on Miriam until she realized Nancy Sinclair was caring for her. Nancy arrived every afternoon at one and left at four o'clock. She bathed Miriam, gave her needed meds and kept her company. Nancy's mannerisms were gentle and Abigail had to admit she was an excellent nurse. She began to interact easily with Nancy. Abigail had never imagined an Englischer as being a compatible friend.

"Who is that young man getting off his horse?" Nancy asked. "He is very handsome."

"That's Abby's future husband," Mary said. "His name is Seth Weaver."

Abigail was mortified. "Mary, he is not my future husband. He is simply a gut friend to our family." The ten year old grinned and her eyes said the opposite.

Abigail didn't budge to answer the knock on the door. Mary ran to it and swung it open. Seth smiled and told her thank you for letting him inside. He greeted everyone, including Nancy who he called by name. Abigail let that pass since it seemed several Amish members knew who she was.

"I came to speak with your Daed on a matter," Seth said.

"He's in the barn," Mary said. "Come along and I'll show you our new calf."

Seth laughed and followed her outside. Abigail wondered what Seth wanted to see her father about. She saw them looking at an older buggy and decided they talked about repairs needed. Seth's father owned the buggy repair shop in the community so it made sense to her.

"I understand your community is preparing for the big picnic." Nancy spoke to Miriam. "If you plan to go I will be happy to get you ready for it."

Miriam shook her head. "I'm not so sure I'll be up to it this year, Nancy."

"You can let me know tomorrow. If you decide you want to give it a try, I can come in the morning and help Abigail prepare you for it."

Nancy Sinclair eased into the family and soon was invited to partake of some of their family activities. She loved the Amish way of life and the people, but felt she could never live like they did. The work seemed endless and she understood why occasional celebrations came around. She worried about Miriam Bontrager. Her disease progressed and Nancy often consulted with Dr. Andrews on different ways to care for her. When the day came for the picnic, mounds of food had been prepared. Miriam decided against joining the family and accepted Nancy's offer to spend the day with her.

When they arrived at the Wirth farm, Bishop Wirth was setting up tables on the side yard along with the men and boys. The women took their food dishes to the large kitchen and Rachel Wirth directed where they should go. Everyone was in a festive mood. Many asked about Miriam and all assured Abigail her mother was in the best of hands with Nancy Sinclair.

The children played organized games and the teenagers and unmarried young adults sang songs together. Everyone else caught up on the latest news around their community. Seth Weaver joked with Zeke and Aaron. Others joined in playing tricks on one another until dinner was announced. Seth rushed ahead to make sure he sat across from Abigail. He couldn't wait to nab her after the meal and ask her to take a walk with him.

Abigail noticed Seth's eyes danced. She wasn't sure if it was because of the excitement of the gathering or if he was on the verge of teasing her. She shifted when he seemed to keep his eyes on her. Rebekah leaned toward her ear.

"I think Seth is ready to step up, don't you?"

Abigail blushed. "I have no idea what he's up to."

"It's about time is all I have to say."

Seth barely ate his dessert until Aaron reminded him that if he didn't dig in he would eat the generous slice of chocolate cake himself. Seth forked the cake and finished it quickly. Some left the tables to play more games and the women began clearing the tables. He spotted Abigail and kept his eyes on her until she finished helping. He caught up with her as she and Rebekah walked outside.

"Abigail, do you want to take a short walk with me?"

Rebekah nudged her. "Yes, that will be nice," Abigail said. "I need to walk off some of that dinner."

When they were a few yards from the others, Seth stopped.

"Abigail, I have spoken with your father and he has given me permission to court you." His words came from his mouth as if he spoke of general things. Then he realized she may turn him down. "I hope you agree with him."

Abigail hesitated. "I do like you very much, Seth, but I am not so sure you want someone who won't always be available for courtship. I mean it is true Nancy Sinclair has been wonderful but I still worry about my Maem as if it is all still on me."

"I am a patient man, Abigail. I understand your duties toward your Maem and it is a generous thing you do. We can decide the best days for buggy rides. Perhaps at times we can take a picnic snack or lunch to the creek and just enjoy the water."

Abigail smiled and Seth relaxed. "I will be happy to allow you to court me, Seth."

"There is nothing in this world that will make me happier, Abigail. There is no church service this Sunday. Is it all right with you if I come by tomorrow evening?"

"I will look forward to it."

Seth didn't want to go back and join the others. Several knowing eyes landed on them and he suggested they tell the news to everyone.

"I suppose that is a gut idea," Abigail said. "If we don't announce our courtship we will be nagged about it one by one. This way everyone is here and can hear it all at once."

Rebekah was first to hug her friend. She told Seth it took him long enough and he had the grace to scuff his shoes in the dirt with his head down. Reuben watched from where he sat talking with friends about the upcoming harvest season, and he approved.

When everyone arrived home, Abigail gave her mother the news. Miriam's eyes lit up. She told her daughter Seth Weaver was an excellent choice for her future.

"Now can I say he will be her husband?" Mary asked.

Everyone laughed. "Give everything time, Mary," Miriam said.

Nancy was impressed with how much love flowed through the room. She told Abigail congratulations and then gave her a rundown of her day with Miriam. "Enjoy the rest of your evening," Nancy said, "I must be getting home."

"I'll dip some of the stew into a bowl for you to take home with you," Abigail said. "It looks like there is plenty here plus if you'd like some of Ruth's potato salad she left extra in the icebox." Mary piped in that she left some of her slaw as well.

"Thank you. I'll take the stew. It will save me making a late supper for Rob. He is a patient husband but he will definitely enjoy homemade stew like this."

When she drove away Abigail brought out food for the evening meal. The men ate and left for the barn to take care of evening chores. Ruth and Mary helped Abigail clean the kitchen. Mary yawned and sat down on the sofa.

"You can say your prayers tonight at your bedside, Mary. You've have a big day and I'm afraid you'll go sound to sleep and fall off the sofa," Miriam said. She smiled at her youngest daughter who agreed. Mary kissed her mother and told her goodnight.

The next evening as promised, Seth arrived to take Abigail for their first buggy ride together. A wide grin spread across his face. She felt his strong hand clasp hers as he helped her into the buggy. The closeness caused shivers through her body and she forgot the daily chores and care of her ill mother.

4

THE DECISION

Nancy Sinclair arrived Tuesday afternoon right on time as usual. She carried her medical bag and greeted Abigail and Miriam. Ruth and Mary had returned to school and the quiet of the house seemed strange to Nancy. Miriam sat in her wheelchair in the kitchen and chatted with Abigail but other than that the usual laughter from the younger girls was absent.

"It sure is quiet in here," Nancy said.

Abigail laughed. "That's because the noisy ones are in school."

Nancy suggested she bathe Miriam before her nap. Miriam agreed and while Abigail finished the dishes from lunch, Nancy took her patient into the small room off her bedroom. Abigail thought of Seth. She thanked God he was as patient as he promised. He didn't push her to go out too often with him. He understood her duties.

Nancy left at three-thirty on Tuesdays since she helped with patients in Dr. Andrews' office in Valley Falls. This day was no exception. She left just as Ruth and Mary skipped in the back door. Mary bubbled over with news of her day at school while Ruth continued inside shaking her head.

"Mary knows Nancy has to leave early on Tuesdays and yet she can't stop talking."

Abigail smiled. "Nancy keeps walking so I'm sure Mary will get the picture." She poured lemonade for her sisters and set a plate of chocolate chip cookies on the table. Then she rolled her mother into the kitchen and poured a cup of hot tea for her and one for herself. Mary came in as full of energy as if she was starting her day.

"Now, Mary and Ruth, tell us about your day," Miriam said. "You tell your story first, Ruth and then we'll hear Mary's."

Zeke came inside. His forehead furrowed into ridges. "Daed is having trouble with the cow about ready to give birth. I'm going to Amos Graber's and ask him to come and look her over." Amos farmed and had a way with animals, often saving them due to his skills. "Aaron is mending a fence in the back pasture. Daed doesn't want the mare to get out. She finds it hard to be fenced in." Zeke hurried out to get Amos.

Abigail wheeled her mother into the sitting room and asked her if she would like to sit on the front porch.

"Let's pray the cow is fine," Miriam said. "I'll sit in here and read the Bible."

The three sisters and their mother joined hands and prayed for the health of the cow and her unborn calf. Then Abigail went to the bedroom to get her mother's medication. She saw that the bottle was empty. Nancy failed to tell them her mother was running low on that one med. Abigail told her mother about it.

"I'm so sorry, Abigail. Nancy told me the other day it was getting low and I completely forgot to tell you."

"Dr. Andrews said you shouldn't miss a dosage at all," Abigail said. "I'll go out and ask Daed if Aaron can go into town to refill it. The drug store won't close for another hour and a half."

Reuben looked up expecting to see Amos Graber. He gave a crooked smile to Abigail.

"Daed, Maem has no medicine left that she is supposed to take now. She forgot that Nancy told her the bottle was almost empty the other day. Can Aaron go into town to get it refilled?"

"You'll have to go, Abigail. I'll saddle the horse for you. Aaron has to get that fence mended or we'll lose that restless mare. I can't leave this cow now."

Abigail froze. "Maybe Zeke can go when he gets back."

"He may be needed here. If not, he has to take one of the horses and go pick up the repaired buggy at the Weaver place. We'll need it for an extra in case your mother has an emergency."

Abigail had no other solutions. Her father saddled her horse and she rode off into town after telling her mother where she was going. Everything seemed to happen at once, she thought. Surely she could go directly to the drug store, pick up the prescription and get back home as soon as possible.

She breathed easier when she saw that the store had only a few customers in it. She was second in line at the prescription counter. The Druggist recognized Miriam's name on the script and asked Abigail how she was doing. Abigail answered in a general way and appreciated his concern. She paid for the medication and left the store. She had tied her horse to the post at the end of the block and though a few yards away it seemed miles to reach it. The sun dipped behind the buildings causing the day to appear ending sooner than normal along the shaded street. She reminded herself she was not in the open countryside. Lost in thoughts of her peaceful surroundings at home, she was startled when she heard arguing.

Voices rose and fell from the narrow alleyway between two shops. Just a few feet more and she would be safely on her horse, she thought. The yelling became louder. She glanced into the alley as she passed its entrance. Tyler Johnson berated his younger brother Tim. Matt Kilgore stood back and egged Tyler on.

"Do it, Tyler. You can get rid of the pest once and for all. He'll never tell tales about you to your father again."

Tyler cursed at his younger brother. Abigail stood still, unable to move or to take her eyes from the scene. She saw abject fear in Tim's eyes as they darted from Matt and back to his older brother.

"I didn't mean anything by it, Tyler. Let me go and I won't tag along again."

The more he begged the angrier Tyler became. Abigail gasped when she saw the sharp knife in his right hand. Tyler staggered a little and then regained control. Matt handed him an opened liquor bottle.

"Here, Tyler, take another drink. That should steady you."

Tim struggled to get rid of his brother's strong grasp. Abigail's hand flew to her mouth and as if in slow motion she watched Tyler Johnson thrust the knife into his brother's chest. Tim fell against the nearby wall and slumped to the ground in the alley. Matt ran to the opposite end of the passageway. Tim turned toward the sidewalk where Abigail stood staring in horror. Tyler wiped the knife on his jeans and pushed it into the hip holder. Cruel and threatening eyes locked onto Abigail's face as he reached for the knife again. Her heart pummeled against her chest. Sure that she would be his next victim she put her hands up in defense.

Tyler stopped and reinserted the knife when several straggling shoppers walked by. They were in deep conversation oblivious to their immediate surroundings. When they were out of earshot, she smelled the stale odor of a pungent substance on his breath. She wanted to shout for help but no words found their way through her constricted throat.

Tyler glanced right and left and saw another pedestrian approaching.

"I know who you are," Tyler said in a low voice. She stepped back to get away from his foul breath. "If you breathe a word of any of this I will give you the same treatment. You won't be safe from now on. Remember that." He swung around and staggered off in the opposite direction.

Abigail realized she had forgotten to pray for her safety during the horrific ordeal. She praised God for taking her safety into His hands. She wanted to take a look at Tim Johnson but didn't dare. She attempted three times to mount her horse and even when successful her mind was in turmoil. How could she leave that boy lying in the alley saturated with blood? He was hurt badly and needed help. The revulsion she felt that his own brother could harm him caused her stomach to turn over and she quickly coaxed her horse around and spurred it to a fast gallop. She held the bile from escaping until she reached the first sign of the countryside. She stopped her horse and leaned over to rid herself of the poison that arose within her.

She fought her internal battle as to whether she should go back and help Tim, or hope someone else would come to his aid. It took the vivid memory of Tyler Johnson's threat to make her decision.

The horse sped into the yard and on to the barn. Abigail got off it before it stopped. Amos Graber came from the barn and looked at Abigail and then at her horse.

"You'll have to rub that horse down. It looks like she's had quite a ride."

Abigail clutched her hands into a fist to steady them. "I'll do that. It's been a while since she's had a gut run like that." She went into the barn to get a towel off the hook. Her father told her the cow was going to be fine. Rubbing down her horse helped calm Abigail outwardly, but inside she shook uncontrollably. She hurried inside to give her mother the needed medicine.

"Are you all right, Abigail?" Miriam asked. "I know town isn't your favorite place to go. I do appreciate what you did for me."

Abigail assured her mother she was fine. She turned away to retrieve two pills and tried to stabilize her trembling hands.

Reuben came inside to give the good news about the cow to his wife. Abigail's face was ashen and taut with an emotion he didn't recognize. He knew it wasn't normal for her.

"Are you all right, daughter?" he asked.

"I am fine. I have Maem's pills ready. She should take them

right away since I am over an hour late with them." She focused on her hands.

Reuben and Miriam exchanged glances. Worry stood out on their faces.

"Let's pray thanksgiving for the healthy cow and for the safe trip to and from town that Abigail just completed." Reueben bowed his head and prayed the prayers. Abigail tried to engulf her thoughts in his words. She felt her mother's hand squeeze tighter than usual in hers.

By the time she sank into her bed Abigail's entire demeanor crashed. She allowed her body to shake and the tremors shot through her as if an earthquake set off inside her. She prayed fervently for strength and direction. Tim Johnson's inert body and the seeping blood invaded her consciousness. The clock on her table read three in the morning before she fell into a restless sleep.

Her parents were alarmed at her appearance at breakfast. Dark circles had formed under her eyes. She mechanically cooked and served breakfast. Ruth made lunches for herself and Mary. They kissed their parents good-bye and started for school. Zeke and Aaron went to the barn to begin morning chores. Reuben knew he needed to check on the cow again and he told Miriam and Abigail he would see them mid-morning. Abigail nodded. Reuben gave his wife a silent message to find out what troubled their daughter.

Abigail carried out her tasks and cared for her mother as usual. Miriam decided to give her time. Dinner was served at noon and when her brothers and father left to go back to chores, she cleared the table and waited for Nancy Sinclair to arrive.

"Why don't you go and see Rebekah this afternoon, Abigail?

Nancy will be here at any moment and I'll be fine until she comes."

"I'll wait until she gets here. Then maybe I will ride over to see Rebekah."

One o'clock came and went. Nancy did not show up. When two o'clock arrived Miriam wondered aloud what was keeping her nurse.

"Perhaps she had an emergency at Dr. Andrews' office," Abigail said. "I'll give you your next medication and read to you for a while. Or if you feel tired I'll help you get into bed." Abigail was glad that she made the decision to stay with her mother until the nurse arrived.

When three o'clock rolled around and still no Nancy, Abigail reassured her mother that Nancy must have a good reason not to come. "She has been very faithful. Perhaps she is ill and hasn't sent word yet."

"I hope she isn't sick," Miriam said. "She is so kind and loving. If she doesn't come in soon, then you should go over to the Grabers' farm and use their emergency telephone. You could call Dr. Andrew's office and inquire."

"I'm sure she will be here tomorrow."

When the third day arrived and Nancy had not shown up to relieve Abigail, the whole family worried about her. Abigail agreed to call the doctor's office and ask about her. In the meantime, Rebekah arrived for a visit that afternoon. She joined Abigail and her mother for lemonade on the front porch. After they talked of community happenings, Rebekah said something that shook Abigail to the bone.

"Did you hear about the tragedy of the Johnson family?" The women shook their heads in the negative. "Their youngest

31

son Tim was found in an alley on Main Street. He had been stabbed to death."

Abigail turned white and ran from the porch. When she turned around the corner of the house she lost everything she had eaten that day. She knew Tim's injuries had been serious but she didn't expect him to die. Then she recalled the amount of blood and Tyler's words. It hit Abigail that Tyler knew his brother was already dead when he threatened her.

The notion she was a witness to a murder of an Englischer caused more upheaval in her stomach. She felt Rebekah's hand on her shoulder.

"I'm sorry, Abigail. I didn't mean to give you news that would upset you like this. Tim was their youngest son and loved by everyone. They have no idea who did this to him but I'm sure they will find the person responsible." She was shocked at the expression on Abigail's face. "Are you all right? Perhaps you should lie down."

Rebekah couldn't figure out why her friend was that upset over the unfortunate turn of events. She felt sorry for the Johnsons but she was sure Abigail didn't know them personally.

They walked back around to the porch where her mother sat. Concerned spread across her mother's face and Abigail regretted she upset her. Miriam's illness took enough of a toll on her without Abigail causing more harm.

"I'm sorry, Maem, I was shocked at the news. The Johnsons are a lovely and gut family."

"I understand," Miriam said. She recalled how upset her daughter had been since she returned from her emergency trip into town. Surely what happened didn't relate in any way to the unexpected death of the young boy. "We must pray for the family."

"Is Nancy still working out for you?" Rebekah asked. She felt the need to change the subject.

"She was doing a fine job of caring for me. She relieved Abigail considerably," Miriam said. "However, she hasn't been here for the last few days. We are worried she may be ill. Now that you've given us this news perhaps she is needed for the Johnson family."

"There was a sign on the General Store that it will be closed until further notice," Rebekah said. "My Maem and I were in town yesterday and didn't see Nancy around. She has a gut reputation for her nursing skills. I'm sure she will be back soon."

Two evenings later Seth Weaver stopped to pick Abigail up for a buggy ride. The early fall air was crisp and he made sure he had an extra blanket along. She smiled at him once they were settled in but she appeared tired.

"Let's go to the creek and listen to the soothing water," Seth said.

Abigail agreed. "The waters are calming. They are so constant and their motions are ever the same." She yearned for the peace the stream held for itself. She had been in turmoil ever since she heard about Tim Johnson's death at the hands of his own brother. She had told no one of what she had witnessed.

Seth spread an old blanket beneath the elm tree and they sat down. The brook sent reassuring messages to Abigail. Seth asked her if it had helped to have Nancy Sinclair take part of the load from her.

"It definitely did help me and my Maem, too. She is a wonderful caregiver but she hasn't been here for several days. We don't know if she is ill or what has happened. We've had no word from her at all."

"I knew Nancy before she married. She took care of my grandmother soon after she got her license to practice nursing. Nancy Johnson was a gut nurse from the day she graduated from nursing school until today. I was so sorry to hear about her brother's death. I'm sure that's why she hasn't come to care for your Maem."

Abigail stared at him. The full realization that Nancy Sinclair was Tyler's and Tim's sister hit her hard. "I had no idea she was the daughter of the General Store owners. Do they know who killed her brother?" Abigail forced the bile down and swallowed hard.

"I have heard there were no witnesses to what happened. They have been trying to locate Tyler but he left town. He's like that from what I understand. He's often in trouble with the law and they figured he did something and is trying to evade getting caught."

Abigail swallowed again. "Maybe we should head back home now."

"I'm sorry, Abigail. I shouldn't have passed gossip on like that. Besides, it's all very disturbing." He reached for her hand. It felt cold and he felt a tremor. "I'm so sorry I upset you."

"I'm fine, Seth. It's been a long day. We had no idea Nancy

was the slain boy's sister. We must pray for her and the family."

Seth agreed and before they left for home, he bowed his head and prayed prayers of healing and praise. Abigail knew she had no choice other than to tell someone the truth. If the same thing had happened to Zeke or Aaron she shuddered to think how she would feel and the effect it would have on her parents. She would visit Bishop Wirth early the next morning.

Seth felt better that Abigail chatted more going home than she had at the beginning of their ride. He joined in with a few jokes and by the time he told her goodnight, he knew she felt better.

Reuben and Miriam breathed sighs of relief when they heard Abigail humming a tune while she cooked breakfast. It was Saturday and her sisters were home from school for the weekend. She asked Ruth if she would watch after their mother.

"I have an errand to run and will be back in an hour. Can you do this for me?"

"I know how to take care of Maem. I'll do everything carefully."

Miriam laughed softly. "I don't break either. Ruth is a gut caregiver. Whatever you have to do, Abigail, go and do it." When her daughter left, she prayed silently for her.

5

THE TRUTH

A bigail rode to the Parsonage. Rachel Wirth opened the door and invited her inside. She went into her husband's study to tell him he had a visitor. He was surprised and pleased to see Abigail Bontrager. He closed the door behind them and told her to sit down.

"I must tell you something I witnessed in Valley Falls several days ago." She took a deep breath. "It is about the Englisch boy who was found in the alley."

Bishop Wirth's head jerked up. "What about it?"

"I know who killed him. I saw it all happen." She twisted her fingers together. "The alley was shadowed but I know who did it."

"How did you get a gut look at the person if it happened in the darkened alley?"

"He came out into the fading light. He stood a foot from me and threatened me if I told anyone what I had witnessed."

She clasped her hands together to keep them still. "I am telling you the truth, Bishop. I don't know what to do."

Bishop Wirth leaned back in his chair. He tried to shake the shock of her news off. "The Englisch believe that it is right to judge others through their court system. Amish do not believe any judgment can be passed other than from Gott. It is not our custom to be in the middle of Englisch laws."

"What about the truth of what I know? The family is grieving not knowing what really happened to their young son. The man who killed him was his own brother."

Silence fell heavy in the room while the Bishop thought about her words. "Where is the man who took his brother's life?"

"I have heard he has left town. He apparently has been in trouble before and his family thinks he ran from the Englisch Law because of something else he has done. They have no idea it was their older son Tyler Johnson who killed his brother."

The Bishop's eyes bored into Abigail's face. "Where have you heard gossip like that, Abigail? I am surprised you have indulged in such things."

"I didn't pursue the matter. I was told that information. My interest is solely in what I witnessed. I feel I should speak up."

"I will gather the Elders and we will decide what is best in the matter." He dismissed Abigail and told her to pray over the events and to ask God to forgive the person who committed the deed.

Instead of feeling relief, Abigail felt more confused. Once again she put herself in the shoes of Tim Johnson's family.

She would want to know who did it. As an Amish woman she would then leave the judging in the hands of her God but no matter what, she would want to know. She wondered where Tyler was. She glanced several times toward the tree line across the road from her family home and prayed he wasn't there watching her every move. Would she be in more danger if she confessed to the Englisch Law Officers? More importantly, how could she live her life with the knowledge on her conscience?

Reuben watched Abigail unsaddle her horse. Though she had seemed happy and relaxed at breakfast she was once more tensed up. He couldn't allow her to continue this way. Something had happened the evening she went into town to the drug store and he was determined to find out what it was. He called her over to him.

"Abigail, you must tell me what is bothering you. At first, I thought it was fatigue but I am sure it is more than that. Something has upset you and you can't go on like this."

Tears formed in her eyes and she fought to keep them at bay. She felt her father's arms enfold her. "I have something terrible on my mind, Daed. I just saw Bishop Wirth and I don't feel he helped me at all."

She told Reuben the story of the evening she witnessed Tim Johnson's murder in the alley at the hands of his wayward brother. Reuben's heart seemed to stop beating. Abigail had more to tell him. She related that Seth mentioned in passing that Nancy Sinclair had the last name Johnson before her marriage to Rob Sinclair.

"She is Tyler Johnson's brother. She doesn't know he is the one who took the life of her beloved young brother. It all answers why she hasn't come back to help us."

Reuben pulled her closer. "My daughter, you are carrying a very heavy burden. We will wait to find out what the Bishop and Elders decide. In the meantime, we will pray that Gott will bless you and make you secure in His care."

Abigail relaxed and stepped back while she and her father bowed their heads in prayer. She thanked him for his support and then returned to her mother. Abigail was happy to be distracted by Ruth who reported everything she had done for her mother. When Ruth and Mary went outside, Abigail told Miriam the reason Nancy had not come to work in the last few days.

"That is terrible," Miriam said. "I am sure she is suffering along with the rest of her family. We must keep them all in our prayers."

Abigail vowed she wouldn't upset her mother by telling her she was a witness to the horrible event that affected Nancy Sinclair and her family. If Nancy did return to care for her mother she felt their friendship would be severed as a result of what Abigail witnessed and kept to herself.

Word spread through the Amish community that Tim Johnson's body had been laid to rest. A week later, Nancy Sinclair drove into the Bontrager dirt driveway. She apologized for not letting them know why she hadn't fulfilled her promise to Miriam and Abigail.

"It was all such a shock that I haven't been able to focus on anything."

They told her how sorry they were for her loss and understood her absence. In the meantime, Abigail grew restless as she waited to hear the final word from Bishop Wirth regarding what she should do. One evening the Bishop arrived at their home and told Reuben and Abigail he wished to speak to them in private. Miriam's eyes held questions but she didn't ask them. The three walked outside and talked.

"The Elders and I have concluded that you should leave things as they are. In time the memories will fade from your mind. The young boy is at peace and in Gott's presence. That is what is most important in the matter."

"What about the brother who took his life?" Abigail asked. "Is he meant to walk free and be given the chance to act that way again?"

Reuben touched her arm to calm her.

"Everything is in Gott's hands, Abigail," Bishop Wirth said.

"I cannot live my life in peace if the scene I witnessed continues to remain within me. I must confess what I witnessed. It is the only way."

The Bishop shook his head. "You asked for my advice. I am following the Amish rules of life. We aren't the judges of anyone. Only Gott can do that."

"I'm not judging. I simply want to do what is right and then let it go."

Reuben stepped in. He sensed a row between his daughter and the Bishop neared. "We honor your direction, Bishop, but I must side with Abigail. She is carrying a heavy burden that is too much for her. I will go with her to the Englisch Sheriff's department and allow her to tell what she knows."

"I am against that," Bishop Wirth said, "but if you have made up your minds then it is on you. The rest of the community will look unfavorably on your decision. Your actions will be deemed very serious." He turned and walked away. Father and daughter stood still until the last of the hoof beats could be heard.

"We must first tell your Maem what is going on. Then tomorrow you will tell the Sheriff. I will be by your side."

Abigail managed to nod her head. For the first time in days Abigail slept a full night and awoke rested. Her mother had taken the news with deep concern but agreed the decision was the right one.

Zeke rode to Rebekah's the next morning and asked her if she could sit with Miriam since his father and sister had business in town. Ruth and Mary were in school. Rebekah gladly agreed.

Reuben bowed his head before they started for Valley Falls and prayed. His words comforted Abigail. When they arrived at the Sheriff's office the clerk told them to sit down and she would tell Sheriff Rod Chance they wanted to see him. The Sheriff thought this wouldn't take long since the Amish rarely had problems that demanded action from his department. Sheriff Chance invited them to sit down. He began by mentioning upcoming harvests on the Bontrager farm. He hoped to relax them, especially the young woman.

"I know you didn't come in to chat about farm work, Mr. Bontrager. How may I help you?" Sheriff Chance liked the Amish and made sure his people mingled in amiable ways with their Amish neighbors. He did not tolerate ill treatment of them.

"My daughter has some important information we feel you should know about." Reuben introduced Abigail.

Sheriff Chance noted the flawless pale skin of the young woman who sat across from him. Her deep blue eyes caught him off-guard. He encouraged her to tell him what was on her mind.

Abigail took a deep breath and told him the story of what she had witnessed. Sheriff Chance moved forward and gave her his full attention. He didn't ask why she waited this long to confess what she had seen. He knew the Amish shunned anything that had to do with the court system. He asked her specific questions and ended with one that caused Abigail to shiver in fear.

"Did Tyler Johnson threaten you in any way when he got that close to you?"

Abigail nodded her head. In a soft voice she recounted his exact words.

"We know where he is. He disappeared about the same time of his brother's death and two days ago returned here. Everyone thought he was running from another one of his petty crimes perhaps in a nearby town. Now I know why he got away so fast."

Reuben and Abigail sat still while Sheriff Chance pushed a button on his telephone and ordered a Deputy to pick up Tyler Johnson.

"Read him his rights and tell him he is being arrested for the murder of his brother Tim Johnson. Pick up Matt Kilgore while you're at it on the same charge. Take three Officers with you and radio for more help if you need it."

"Will Abigail have to testify in your courtroom?" Reuben's eyes begged the Sheriff to spare his daughter.

"We may be able to arrange for a taping of her testimony in private. I will see what I can do."

Reuben thanked the Sheriff. A few minutes later they got into their buggy just as Tyler Johnson was marched into the Precinct in handcuffs. He locked eyes briefly with Abigail before she turned her head away from him.

The next day when Nancy came to care for her mother, Abigail told the nurse she must talk with her before she began. They sat in the sitting room while her mother read her Bible in her bedroom.

"Nancy, I have something I must tell you. I have prayed the shock won't be too great for you and I want to apologize for not stepping forward sooner. It would have spared your family grief about who may have taken your sweet brother's life."

Nancy held her breath. What could this meek Amish woman know about Tim's death that no one else had knowledge of? The nurse knew her brother had been arrested for something but she had worked the night at the hospital and didn't know what the charge was at this point.

Abigail's fingers twitched in her lap and she began her story as told several times before. She searched Nancy's face for a reaction when she finished. When no words were spoken, Abigail decided to tell her the last part. "My father went with me yesterday to the Sheriff's Office in town. I told him everything I witnessed. Your brother has been arrested for the deed."

Abigail prayed the look on Nancy's face was one of acceptance but she couldn't be sure. Nancy stood up and walked to the window. After a few minutes she turned to Abigail.

"I don't understand the ways of the Amish people or how you think. I don't know why you are just now coming forth." She paced a few steps. "My brother hated Tim but Tyler hated just about everyone he came in contact with, even our parents who have shown only good toward him. He has been in and out of jail on lesser counts." She wiped a tear from her eye. "He had no reason to kill Tim. Even if he had beaten him up I'd understand that coming from him, but murder? There is no excuse for that."

Abigail attempted to explain why she hadn't come forth sooner but even to her the words sounded hollow. Miriam wheeled herself into the room.

"We are so sorry about all of it, Nancy. We will understand if you don't want to continue working here."

Nancy looked at them. "I may need a few days to process all of this but if you will have me, I will continue to help you." She wiped her eyes with the back of her hand again. Abigail handed her a clean handkerchief from her pocket and Nancy accepted it with a weak smile. "I guess the good of it all is that Tyler won't be on the streets to hurt anyone else. Thank you, Abigail, for coming forth with the truth."

That evening Seth Weaver found Abigail on the front porch laughing with her sisters. He ruffled Mary's hair when she said, "Here comes your future husband, Abby."

Abigail couldn't wait to take her ride away from her sisters. She wrapped the light cloak around her shoulders and got into the buggy. On the ride down the road she told Seth everything. He wanted to take her into his arms and kiss the pain away. Knowing it wouldn't be proper he reached for her hand and held it tightly. Abigail savored his touch.

"I knew something was bothering you, Abigail. I am glad that part is over for you. Will you have to stand in an Englisch courtroom?"

"I won't have to do that. It has been arranged for me to answer questions privately behind closed doors and they will record what I say. I think the Sheriff said it will be played in the courtroom whatever that means."

"It means they will hear your voice but won't see you."

They rode in silence for a quarter of a mile. Seth stopped the horse on the edge of the road and turned to Abigail.

"Abigail, if your father approves, will you marry me?"

Her heart leapt to her throat. "I strongly doubt my father will object. And my answer is yes."

"We will plan for next year. Your father mentioned some extra land of his. Perhaps my father can purchase a part of it from him for us. You would live close enough to continue to look after your Maem if you would like that."

"You've thought things out well, Seth. Just remember that once we start our own family we will have to hire Nancy full time."

"That's what I call planning ahead," Seth said. They laughed and continued plans for their future. "How many children do you want?"

"How many will we need? If the farm grows we'd better have plenty of help." Seth teased her about misconstruing the reasons for having children. "I thought I'd get the jump on you when it comes to teasing, Seth." She looked at the clear sky that displayed an array of stars. "We will have as many children as Gott sends us."

Seth took her hand and encouraged the horse to move forward.

Read The Saga of the Amish Sisters Boxset Today

THANK YOU FOR READING

IF YOU HAVE NOT ALREADY DONE SO,
DON'T FORGET TO GET YOUR FREE
BONUS BOOKS. IT IS OUR WAY OF
SAYING THANK YOU FOR BEING ONE OF
OUR TREASURED READERS...

Click Here To Download Your Copy of Grace Abounding

75785018R00033

Made in the USA
Middletown, DE
07 June 2018